GRAMPA-LOP

Written By:
STEPHEN COSGROVE

Illustrated By:
ROBIN JAMES

GROLIER ENTERPRISES INC.
Danbury, Connecticut

A Serendipity Book

Copyright© 1981 by Price/Stern/Sloan Publishers, Inc.
Published by Price/Stern/Sloan Publishers, Inc.
410 North La Cienega Boulevard, Los Angeles, California 90048

ISBN: 0-8431-0586-0

Dedicated to an old man whom I remember but never knew in Metaline Falls, who was my Wizard of the Wood.

Stephen Cosgrove

Deep within the forest of dreams lies a gnarled thicket of wood. The branches fold out far above to form a rich green umbrella that protects all the creatures that live here from the crystal spring showers of early April and May. The rains fall for an hour, maybe two, and then the sun, with rays like golden ribbons at a county fair, streams through the leaves to the ground below.

It was in this thicket that the rabbits of the forest lived and played all their lives. There were rabbits with big fluffy tails and rabbits with barely any tails at all — short ones, fat ones, skinny ones, fluffy ones, and one very old rabbit called Grampa-Lop.

Grampa-Lop was so old that his fur had long since turned to grey. He wore a tattered scarf wrapped around his neck, and always carried a twisted stick that he used for a cane.

Every afternoon at about two or three, Grampa-Lop would sit on his favorite stump and enjoy the warmth of the sun. He would sit quietly until — without his noticing — all the young rabbits would gather around his feet. They would try to be quiet, but it was so hard that a couple of them had to stuff their ears in their mouth to keep from laughing.

Grampa-Lop would lean back on the stump, look around, and begin in a very soft, low voice: "Once upon a time, in the land of mist and magical things, there was an enchanted forest . . ."

As he would slowly tell the tale, a very strange and wondrous thing would happen. Grampa-Lop would begin to stand straighter and straighter. The sunlight would flash from his brown eyes and sparkle throughout the forest. And his fur would glow.

The little rabbits would be totally enchanted as he recounted his tale, because suddenly the very old Grampa-Lop would become the Wizard of the Wood. Most of the rabbits would get so caught up in the story itself that they wouldn't even know that he had finished. He would have to say, "Now, little bunnies, it's time you were on your way." And with that they would scamper back to the thicket in the wood.

Now, the older rabbits were becoming more and more concerned about the little ones. One day, after the little bunnies had disappeared as usual, the older rabbits all gathered together at the thicket.

"I wonder where they go?" they asked themselves. "Every day they disappear at the same time."

"I bet they go off and see that old, useless rabbit, Grampa-Lop," said one. "I just know they're up to no good!"

They chittered and chattered for a while and then decided that when the little rabbits returned that afternoon they would find out exactly what was going on.

Sure enough, right on schedule, the little rabbits returned and, as agreed, the older rabbits asked where they had been.

"Well," one said, "we went into the forest to see Grampa-Lop and he told us a wondrous story of the woods. When he told us the story, the most wonderful, magical thing happened. Grampa-Lop became the Wizard of the Wood!"

"I knew it!" fumed one of the older rabbits. "That old rabbit is teaching these kids nothing but a pack of lies."

"But it's true!" chorused the little rabbits. "When he tells us stories, stars and sparks appear. It's magic."

The older rabbits hopped off to one side and muttered to each other, occasionally looking over their shoulders. Finally, they stormed back to the children.

"We've decided that you are lying because there is no such thing as magic. For that you are to go to bed right this instant, with no supper, and from now on you are forbidden to see this Grampa-Lop ever again!"

With tears streaming from their eyes, the bunnies all shuffled off to their beds. They had heavy hearts and very empty stomachs.

The next day, as usual, Grampa-Lop sat on his favorite stump, soaking up the warm sunshine and waiting for the little rabbits to appear. He sat, and he sat, and he must have dozed off, for he woke with a start as the sun was just about to set. Much to his amazement, there were no baby bunnies, none whatsoever.

"Maybe they forgot," he thought, "but surely they'll remember tomorrow." With that, he hobbled off to his burrow in the wood.

The next day and the next, a saddened Grampa-Lop waited and waited for the children who never came. Finally, in desperation, he began hopping towards the thicket in the wood, searching for some sign of the bunnies.

As he hobbled down the twisted path, leaning heavily on his cane, he came upon one of the older rabbits.

"Good day to you," he said as he bowed stiffly. "I'm looking for all the little rabbits of the wood. You see, I used to tell them stories but they've stopped coming to see me."

"A good thing, too!" snorted the older rabbit. "All those bunnies ever learned from you was to lie and tell their own stories."

Grampa-Lop was shocked. "But I never taught them to lie," he said. "I only told them the wondrous and magical tales of the forest.

"You won't anymore," huffed the rabbit as he hopped quickly back to the thicket.

With a tear trickling down his cheeks, a much older and sadder Grampa-Lop went back to his burrow in the wood.

With nothing to occupy his days now, Grampa-Lop wandered aimlessly about the forest. Once or twice he even went to the thicket in the wood, but as soon as he appeared, the older rabbits would herd the little bunnies to the opposite side.

"Go away!" they shouted. "Old, old rabbits aren't wanted in our thicket." With that, all the rabbits scurried to their burrows.

All alone, Grampa-Lop would hop away from the thicket and return to his part of the woods.

The baby bunnies did as they were told, but they could never forget the magic of the Wizard of the Wood. Sometimes, when they were all alone, they would whisper about how much fun it had been, but most of the time they would just shuffle about the thicket, making dust and feeling very sad.

The older rabbits tried to cheer them up, and sometimes they would even tell a story; but it just wasn't the same.

It got so bad that the little bunnies began to bicker among themselves. It would start innocently with one bunny bumping another bunny, but it always ended in a tangle of arms, legs, and ears as they wrestled on the ground.

Finally, some of the older rabbits couldn't stand it any more and called all the rabbits together.

"This has got to stop," they said. "With all this moping and bickering, nothing is getting done. Food isn't being collected, new burrows aren't being built, and winter's coming."

"If we could just hear the magical stories of Grampa-Lop," said one of the bunnies, "we wouldn't get into so much trouble."

"But there is no such thing as magic!" fumed the older rabbits. "You lied about that before."

"We didn't lie. We told you the truth, and if you'd go with us we'd show you that there really is magic."

The older rabbits thought for a moment and then decided. "We will indeed go with you to your Wizard of the Wood, if only to prove that there is no such thing as magic."

They all hopped into the forest and down the long, twisty trail to the stump where Grampa-Lop sat waiting. He sat as he had always sat, sunning himself and gazing softly into the sky. The little bunnies quickly sat at his feet, while the older rabbits sat disbelievingly on an old, rotting log.

Grampa-Lop leaned back and, with a gleam in his eye, began in a very soft, low voice: "Once upon a time in a land of mist and magical things there was an enchanted forest . . ."

The older rabbits looked on in wonder as Grampa-Lop began to stand straighter and straighter. The sunlight began to flash from his bright brown eyes as he told the tale, and sparkles of magic began to twinkle in the forest around them. As the story wore on, his fur turned from grey to silver, and he truly became the Wizard of the Wood.

All the rabbits, young and old, were totally enchanted as the story came to a beautiful ending. The moment was so beautiful, some of the older rabbits even had tears in their eyes.

No one said a word, so afraid were they to break this magical spell; but one by one they rushed to Grampa-Lop and hugged him with all the love in their hearts.

The older rabbits never apologized for the wrong they had done the bunnies and Grampa-Lop, for everyone knew that sometimes even older rabbits make mistakes, too. But every day now, at exactly the same time, all the rabbits hop from the thicket and rush to listen to Grampa-Lop become the Wizard of the Wood.

LISTEN TO THE OLDER ONES,
THEIR GOLDEN STORIES TRUE;
THEN REMEMBER GRAMPA-LOP
AND THE MAGIC HE SHOWED YOU.